The NIGHT HORSE

With wonderous warm wishes

April Halprin Wayland

1992

The NIGHT HORSE

by April Halprin Wayland *Illustrated by Vera Rosenberry*

SCHOLASTIC INC. / New York

Many thanks to Myra Cohn Livingston
for the "poetry scales,"
for your kindness,
for your belief.

—A.H.W.

Library of Congress Cataloging-in-Publication Data

Wayland, April Halprin.
The night horse / by April Halprin Wayland.
p.   cm.
Summary: A neon-blue horse carries a girl into the night sky,
where she picks a bouquet of stars and feeds them to her steed.
ISBN 0-590-42629-X (hardcover)
[1. Night–Fiction. 2. Horses–Fiction.] I. Title.
PZ7.W35126Ni 1991
[E]–dc20

12 11 10 9 8 7 6 5 4 3 2 1   1 2 3 4 5 6/9

Printed in the U.S.A.   36

First Scholastic printing, February 1991

Designed by Tracy Arnold

Last night I did not sleep at all. I listened from my bed.
I knew the sound. I knew it, but things jumbled in my head.

Outside, the leaves were pounded by a strong, steady rain.
I watched the branches moving in the wind: a tangled mane.

The rain was pounding, pounding — I thought I saw a horse.

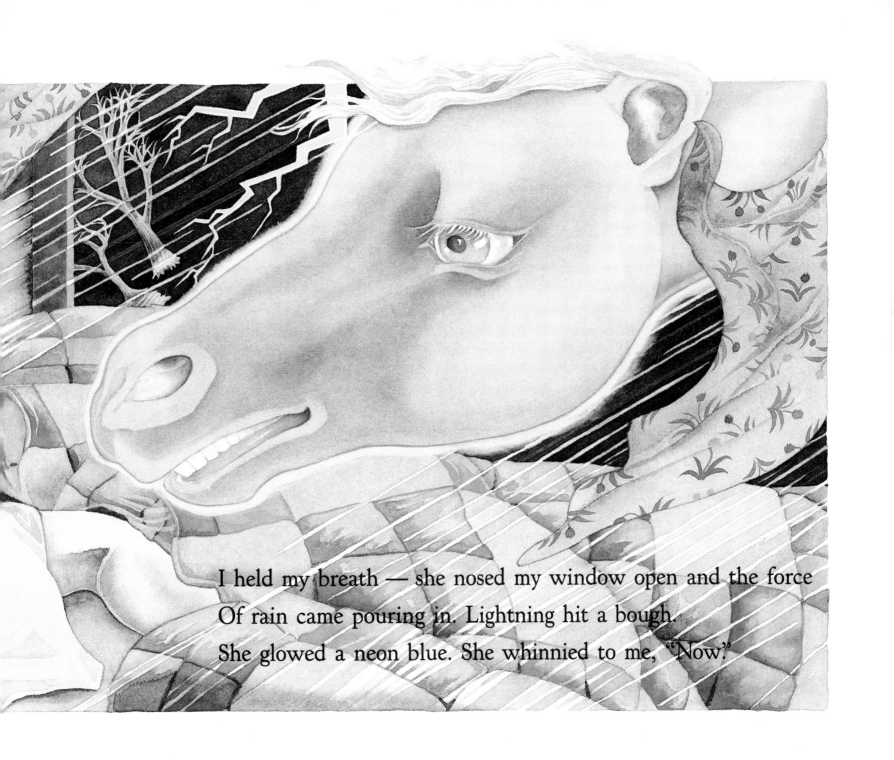

I held my breath — she nosed my window open and the force
Of rain came pouring in. Lightning hit a bough.
She glowed a neon blue. She whinnied to me, "Now."

I mounted her. My bare feet felt the mist upon her side.

I knew it was just rain; still, I hugged her neck to ride.

We passed my parents' window; our dog outside on guard

Howled up. We flew! We soared above the darkened yard.

I knew it was just rain; I knew I slept in bed,
Until I felt the wind, until this blue horse said:

"I am a Blue Night Horse — I've galloped forty years today.
So, I will rest ... and you may pick a star jasmine bouquet."

I tried to wake up in my room. I knew it was just rain.
But the fragrance of the jasmine kept me on the starry plain,
Where other nightgowned children scattered all across the sky,
Each child led by a horse; each picking stars, as I.

I saw them. I could not call — the distance was too far.

I was pulled away by perfume to a midnight field of stars.

I picked a thousand white bouquets that I would take back home.

I lay them on a moonlit knoll. Then I began to roam.

The night was changing colors. I thought, "Just one more star."
But when I found the last, another brilliant one not far
Grew up. I picked another and another — each one more amazing.
I wondered where the rain had gone. Then I saw her grazing

On my bouquets! She ate them all. "But why?" I called. "But why?"

Out of breath, I wildly tore across the dawning sky;

I smelled her flowery mouth. She looked at me and said,

"You're here to feed me stars, although you're far away in bed."

Then I heard the rain again as every other mare
Picked up her child and galloped on the colored morning air.

As my Blue Night Horse and I flew off, I saw the last star wane. She left me, gently, in my bed....

I woke....

There was no rain.